Not Just a Book...

Jeanne Willis

Tony Ross

ANDERSEN PRESS

This is not **just** a book.

You can use it as a hat...

... or a **tent** for your **cat**.

It can keep a table steady.

It can prop a floppy teddy.

You can use it as a funnel...

... or a toy train tunnel.

A brick for building towers...

... or a thing for pressing flowers.

A book is never **just a book.**

It can swat away a fly...

... hide your face if you are shy.

Shoo away a scary bear...

... and catch a fairy in mid-air.

Or keep the wasps out of your drink.

They can make you laugh

and weep.

The End

And they can help you go to sleep.

Books can make you really clever...

... and they stay with you forever.
But the very best thing a book can do...

... is to be **read** and **loved** by YOU.